THIS BOOK BELONGS TO

children's choice®

First published in the United States 1988 by Chronicle Books. Copyright ©1985 by Taro Gomi. American text copyright ©1988 by Chronicle Books. All rights reserved. No part of this book may be reproduced in any form without written permission from the publisher.

Library of Congress Cataloging-in-Publication Data

Gomi, Tarō. Bus stops.
  Summary: A bus follows its daily route through the town, discharging and taking on a variety of passengers. Subtext on each page challenges the reader to find objects or people sprinkled throughout the pictures.
[1. Buses—Fiction. 2. Literary recreations] I. Title.
PZ7.G586Bu   1988   [E]   88-10193   ISBN 0-87701-551-1

10 9 8 7 6 5 4 3 2 1

Chronicle Books   San Francisco, California

BUS STOPS
BY TARO GOMI

CHRONICLE BOOKS   SAN FRANCISCO

 A Children's Choice® Book Club Edition from Macmillan Book Clubs, Inc.

The bus stops at the beach.
An artist steps off.

Can you find two sailboats?

The bus stops near an old church.
Two sightseers get off.

Can you find two sailboats?

The bus stops at the edge of town.
A salesman hops off.

Can you find a fisherman?

Can you find an orange car?

The bus stops at a building site.
Four construction workers leap off.

Can you find a bulldozer?

The bus stops downtown.
Busy commuters rush off.

Can you find a fisherman?

The bus stops at the edge of town.
A salesman hops off.

Can you find an orange car?

The bus stops at a building site.
Four construction workers leap off.

Can you find a bulldozer?

The bus stops downtown.
Busy commuters rush off.

Can you find a helicopter?

The bus stops at a fair.
Some children and their parents run off.

Can you find a clown?

The bus stops near a restaurant.
A mechanic dashes off.

Can you find a cow?

The bus stops at a baseball field.
Ten baseball players jog off.

Can you find a girl on a bicycle?

The bus stops at a hospital.
A nurse comes out to meet it.

Can you find a jogger?

The bus stops at the marketplace.
Some shoppers get off.

Can you find a green van?

The bus stops at a junkyard.
No one gets off.

What can you find here?

The bus stops at a movie set.
An actor runs off.

Can you find a horse?

The bus stops in front of a drugstore.
Oops, a woman just missed the bus!

Can you find a man in a gray hat?

The bus stops outside our house.
We get off.

Can you find a dog?

The bus stops at the garage.
The driver steps off.

Can you find a gasoline pump?

Goodnight, bus.